Lake Sider's Dance

by

Phillip An

GW00393553

Acknowledgements

A special thanks to Simon for his untiring help
For Chrishelda, Billy and Gandalf for showing me
glimpses of truth, beauty and goodness.

Copyright © 2022 Phillip Amey

ISBN: 9798795629452

All rights reserved, including the right to reproduce this book, or portions thereof in any form. No part of this text may be reproduced, transmitted, downloaded, decompiled, reverse engineered, or stored, in any form or introduced into any information storage and retrieval system, in any form or by any means, whether electronic or mechanical without the express written permission of the author.

1

All his life he had known that when he grew up, he wanted to be something that was different. Not just a job, but something vocational, something true. Not knowing what that *something* was he had bumbled around from one job to the other. Training schemes and development processes and opportunities had become the norm for him. He had even considered a monastic life. Then he found banking.

He had been a banker for many years now, perhaps too many to remember. Banking for him though was not the 7 till 7 banking that it is for others within the city. The constant drag of fiscal and financial burden, the targets, the corporate strategy etc. No, this was life, and life to be lived and survived. For this banking was not of an ordinary institution or organisation. This was banking "real time" on the miles upon miles of verges that beautify our roads and motorways.

Have you ever been caught in a traffic jam, or pulled up at the end of slip road and just waited, watched?

Look hard, look beyond yourself. There it lay, right in front of you. The world of bankers.

Unbeknown to you and I there are possibly several thousand bankers, just being, just existing. Their world does not cross with ours nor should it. The common denominators that protrude all sections of social groups, even those who are running from themselves, and others just don't exist here.

Bankers don't rely on or need anything, not permission or state handouts, nor specialist social workers to mange them and seek for conformity. No affiliation or allegiance, just nothing, but also everything.

Within the Old Testament there is a fellow by the name of Melchizedek. He is only cited a few times and but the parallels here are about as close as you get. You cannot be born a banker, nor die a banker. You just become a banker for a time then nothing. No Alpha, no Omega. Genealogy does simply not exist.

Time frames and daily patterns used by the rest of us hold no meaning for bankers. No shift patterns or unsocial hours, just necessity around your life. You tend not be visible throughout the day, but that is more a coping strategy than a rule. Bankers think of themselves as a positive but elusive group, rather than a subversive society in hiding. There is a very real but subtle difference; they breathe deeply and openly and not in the shadows of darkness. Get that, and you get what it truly means to be a banker.

The only group that the bankers would hate, should they care to, would be the poncy new-age travellers. Always banging on about being unique and different and alternative. Don't they realise that they have just created their own little social group? Surely being alternative these days is being "normal"?

Bankers tend not have friends nor enemies, well certainly not that they would actively seek on either front.

There is always the possibility of being spotted by a motorist or bored passenger, but usually by the time this has happened, the voyeur starts to question what they thought they saw in that split second, with what they actually saw, just before they open their big mouth in front of others.

The risk of being seen as foolish in front of friends or authorities is probably the biggest defence weapon that bankers have. It's like saying you just saw the Yeti! You see them alright, and they see you. But you are just too pathetic and weak to acknowledge them, whereas they see and know you. Now ask yourself, who is looking in and who is looking out?

I may have so far portrayed an isolated and desolate existence. This may be true of some but certainly not of others. There are indeed many groups of bankers moving about the highways. Think of the nearest motorway to you, then think of a roundabout that transcends that bit of road. Now think about the amount of space or land that is contained within the confines of that roundabout? Huge, really. Now think about how many conventional dwellings that you could erect upon that land. This may be only two or three (depending upon the Housing association!) But now think about how many people could live and move about the same land should you not know that they are there?

Now multiply that figure by the number of banks and verges that you pass just on your journey to work.

An estimated 250,000 people go missing every year in the UK. Obviously, most return home in a very short space of time. But what about the rest? Where do you think these people go? I am not suggesting that there is a vast colony of people that live in these places, indeed that is the beauty of being a banker, you could have splendid isolation for long periods of time which he'd grown to love and hate over the last 15 years or so. However, the surety that you know your local area like "the back of your hand" may lead you to turn your palm over every now and think again!

Where did it all begin? Why are these people who have deserted our norms and conventions living like vagrants or cavemen?

Certainly, the first bankers led themselves to freedom when the M275 was completed in the eighties. Arguably this was perhaps the most southern extension to the motorway system at that time. But I think it more than this. More than being the first. More than being a new fad or trend for others to follow. It was just about being. The eighties were tough for Portsmouth (as in many places) having echoes the cockney-esque post war generations, with the stark reality of still being a dock town and then the juxtaposition of the new yuppie style slicing through every now and again.

It will always be argued that the frustration of living in Portsmouth with the dominance of the monstrous chalk pits led to the feeling of inadequacy. But many great things and many great people have lived and indeed flourished because of the white lady that shines her edifice upon the city.

Try not to think about bankers as being outside you, but within you only dimensionally different. They are neither running from you nor turning their back on the society that they left. They are like passing people on a two-way escalator; you're all moving, just in different directions for different reasons.

If you have ever had the urge or indeed the courage to take all your clothes off and jump in the sea during the day, or mentally pick a fight with a greater mind. Then you are close to being a banker but few ever have the guts to take the leap.

They do not wish to be normalised as those with a disability or those with different orientation such as faith, colour etc. They just wish to be.

"Conversely" is perhaps the most apt word that could be used for the lives of the bankers.

You rely on new resources, fresh things. They rely on your rubbish. You try to prune your garden and calm your weeds. They beg them to grow for cover like wallpaper.

For us, more cars on the roads are abhorrent, for them bliss. More cars, = more roads, = more verges, = more resources, = more roadside cafes, and restaurants who have early morning deliveries that are unattended for long periods of time.

2

Living and indeed thriving off the waste of others may conjure up a picture of dirt, and disease. This could not be further from the truth. Cleanliness really is next to Godliness, well humane existing and creation at least.

Bankers have developed highly advanced techniques for water filtration and nutrient extraction from the waste of others. Now this does not involve stealing from others; that would be a replication of the world they chose not be in.

In fairness this does use some borrowed energy from the new solar panels that are springing up everywhere, and a bit of basic science (but in the grand scheme of things it's not really theft as we know it). Then just hoses and wheel hubs rotating, boiling, and purifying. Hey presto. Water.

Being a banker focuses the mind when it comes to your own health. Your body is no longer a disposal gift that you can abuse and repair at will, like a washing machine. It is the machine; the programming runs the cycle the cycle needs the motor. The motor demands the energy. The energy needs the programme, and so on. One big wash.

Taking liberties with yourself is not a luxury that the banker has. Asthma will kill you, as many bankers know only too well. Funny really, how cars are the greatest resource that the banker has, whilst not actually owning any of them, yet they are biggest threat without ever coming into direct contact.

The fragility of the banker's life is the first thing that hits you every time you open your eyes.

This was highlighted when a group occupying a stretch of the A303 near Illminster found an abandoned baby in a lay by. The baby died within days. It was not that they didn't try, they did. And you can't apply the survival of the fittest rule either. It's just that the banks and verges of the world could not sustain the very basic needs that the baby needed. Now we are talking about skilled and knowledgeable people with every compassion known to man. But they could not generate the God like state as known on the outside. They gave the infant warmth and food, but this was just not enough. The baby was not to be a banker; moreover, the baby had served its earthly purpose and given so much to so many in such a short space of time. He had compared it to a rose. Any experienced good gardener knows that every now and again there are roses that form perfectly in the bud and often show every sign of coming into bloom; and yet it doesn't. Somehow, they just never fully bloom. These beautiful roses are not lesser but preserved in that state of innocence and fragility but still susceptible to the violence of life at the same time.

You see, bankers, see life as relative. You cannot compare years with worth, nor measure contribution to society to demonstrate a value before death. They see human life like that of a car. You travel so far in the car, then get out and walk the rest of the way. This could be a short journey or long haul. It doesn't matter. You took the journey and served the purpose. You gave and received, and you know with your own confidence that the next part of the journey is on foot, and that travelling on foot is the most natural, organic, and beautiful way to move.

From this you can see that it would be totally untrue to paint a picture of some idyllic existence, roaming freely around the country in a state of personal euphoria. The life is hard; the breaks are few and far between and the consequences are painful and often. But it gives you something. You have the freedom. Not freedom just to move at will or freedom from conventional thought and

7

governance, but freedom of the self. What is time? What are hours? What are to do lists?

Your worship is to your God and your creed is to benefit others. You apply conscience and cognitive justification to all that you do.

There are no leaders within the realm of bankers, no social groups other than the group itself.

If you move as a banker and you feel right, then you stay. If not, then you move freely and without malice or resentment. It's not to say that the last group or individual were better or worst. Just different. And that's okay, bankers like the rest of us cannot alter our own humanity or weakness, but they can, and do develop a very real choice to further a world that exists by itself and for itself, and unto itself will it answer.

Banking is beautiful. There would be no bankers should the way be too fruitless or too austere. Remember, bankers are not sadists and they do not flagellate.

Imagine lying under a Hawthorn bush on a hot summer's eve. The rush hour has come and gone. The people have moved about their business without even knowing you are there. You have studied them with great care, and you are fairly sure that you could predict their occupation with ease. The foliage is dense and affording you maximum cover. You drift into a sleep of the most perfect nature. It doesn't matter if you snore or stir, who will hear you?

There was one occasion though when he nearly did get caught. He was lying just out of sight in a thicket verge just near a layby where the rolling South Downs give way to the sandier soil in Surrey. There was nothing too unusual until a minibus pulled up carry with it what he could only surmise was a hen party (possibly on its way to London?). It was obvious from the giggling and shrieking that the pre-drinks had done their thing and three scantily clad women got off the bus in frantic fashion and proceeded to make their way into the supposed cover not more than two feet from where he lay. Without any warning whatsoever the skirts were up, and the knickers were down, and he was faced with three of the most beautiful bottoms that he'd ever seen! Obviously being so close to an endless torrent of steaming pee wasn't his idea of fun, but boy those bottoms. He mustered his fortitude and kept as silent as he could; after all this kind of incident would not have gone down well with the police or the judge, but hey, whose transgression was the greatest? His or theirs?

3

As the mantra of the passing cars and vans wakes you, you think, and you think. And the thinking you do has been refined and honed to a beautiful conversation with yourself and your God. You are really talking now. You are not just listening and responding to your own thoughts but engaging fully with all that you are and all that you want to be.

Your thoughts don't have conventional processes of social control. You are not reliant on preordained responses or acceptability. You are truly being and have ascended to that place where you can fully know and fully be known.

As your thoughts return to the here and now, you are not jolted back, or wrenched rudely from your daydream but seamlessly carried. You have retained that same calm of mind and grown from your thoughts. They were not abstract or surreal but living feelings and ideas which will make you more whole.

You return with a greater sense of peace and closeness. Then you remember why you chose banking, or did banking choose you?

Depeche Mode had penned one his favourite songs; *Enjoy the silence*, and it was indeed an art form to enjoy the silence and be comfortable with your own company and within your own skin on the banks. This much cherished silence wasn't apparent at first as there was always the *white noise* of life and cars and the elements to contend with but once he'd deconflicted this in his mind, there was an interior silence that offered solace to his soul and within a very short space of time he found that *words* were indeed *very unnecessary*. He liked Depeche Mode as they spoke to the slightly darker or melancholic side within him; and for him, their music was something of a platform or portal which allowed him, in some way to make sense of his existence. Music was one of the things that he missed from his previous life and he genuinely maintained that he loved every kind of music except bloody jazz! He classed himself as a reasonably articulate person, but he never could stand all the sodding spiralling, wrapped up and presented as an art form. He also knew though, that the playlist in his mind was limited up to the point when he made his new life on the banks. He wondered how much of the music that he liked had stood the test of time and was still being played and how mush had been relegated to the annuls of time? What new music had been produced over the last couple of decades? Was it any good? Would he have liked it? He found these thoughts very comforting as it always gave way to the idea of potential and possibility, that the world could recreate itself in a new way for a new generation and with that in mind there would always be hope.

Finding that all elusive place to live is a miracle. Certainly, many of the verges in the southern area were made out chalk. Now, chalk not only holds moisture and is notoriously hard to excavate, but it also leaves you completely white. Now this is no good when your aim is to remain undetected.

As the group began to spread further in land, it became apparent that you did not have to go too far before the layers of sub soil changed completely. This, however, was only half of the story. As with any new dwelling or estate that is being planned there is consideration given to the local infrastructure, and how this links to the demands of the proposed numbers of inhabitants, medical care, bus routes, schools etc.

Now imagine that your "infrastructure" is not about schools and hospitals but about soil depth and density, foliage, running "free" water, roadways, and cameras.

11

All of these must be right before you can even think about the frequency of verge maintenance, patrol cars, food, and possible solace.

Some of the most successful (success being measured by detection and stativity) have chosen the large roundabouts just below a flyover. You see these are very rarely touched for maintenance as they are serving the purpose of concealment for the Highways Agency. The less you see of the roads and its mechanics, the more you see it as a seamless and pleasant place to be. The less you hear of the roads, the more you are inclined to see them as essentially a good thing.

Now there is psychology at work, and plenty of it. You start off by buying an overpriced car (they tax you). You then put overpriced fuel in the car (they tax you). Next you pay your road fund licence (they tax you) and then next thing will be toll fees and guess what? You've been well and truly taxed.

But the bankers don't care about this, because they've left all this for the big verges, the over-sized expanse either side of the road and a few trees which are designed and planted to change sequentially throughout the seasons. These have been designed to give you a false sense of wellbeing, and you love it.

Bankers couldn't care less; in fact, they live off your delusion.

This is no great underworld order taking place, but there is dialogue, and there are rules. There must be, to be so free and so nomadic and elusive you have known and abide by the most stringent of rules. You may choose to live on your own, but you are responsible to and for the banking world as a whole.

One lapse or mistake and the whole existence of bankers could turn into an urban myth exposed with a focus as big as ufology or crop circles.

-You may not speak to or encourage anyone to be a banker.

-Your allegiance lay with the ideal not any one person.

-You will not steal directly from anyone for anything other than for survival.

-You do not own or belong to the banks, but they are you.

-You will never leave the banks.

These may seem hard, and liberty and freedom may not be apparent, but it's there alright. It could be argued that banking is like autism; you must be within the spectrum of banking to see the truth.

And besides, governance is everything.

Now there are times when the rules can be bent. There was a group moving about the M4 and slip roads who took serious liberties with a lay-by café van. Every Tuesday night they used to "borrow" the guy's TV to watch Derek Acorah on "Most Haunted". Derek by all accounts has taken on a cult status with his ability to see things beyond himself and knowing a presence without using his normal senses. I think he would make a good banker, or a bad motorist!

This is just one example where bankers cross over the worlds and use secular resources for their own ends. But this is on their terms for their benefit. You see, if they had no idea of what was occurring beyond the tarmac then failure and extinction are just moments away.

Take for example the recent security scare when the police thought that someone was going to launch an attack on a plane from its flight path. The bankers heard this and found the guy in bushes just south of the runway. They used the roadside phones and called this in. The guy was rumbled (although he got away) and the disaster was avoided. Had they not known of the risk then most certainly the plane would have been shot down and the banks would have searched and stripped to death?

So, there was a trade off with everyone being a winner (except the scummy murdering terrorist).

Think about how many times you hear a body being found by the side of the road or in a wooded area. You are told that a passing motorist had made the discovery. But they never tell you name or any other details. Why? Because there were no passing motorists. It's the bankers who make the call, when and only when they have passed the word and cleansed the area of all trace.

You will often see the police finding odd bits of clothes deep in the middle of nowhere. Now how do you suppose they get there? It certainly isn't the wind nor is it rubbish. Clothes don't just fling themselves randomly 40 feet in from an embankment. They are usually the remnants of a banker's clothes who got caught short after an incident and had to bolt taking all that they could. The real pisser is that it was probably the banker who called in the incident and then had to try and gather their washing which he was trying to discreetly dry and was left with bugger all after doing you guys a favour.

Every now and again the authorities do find a banker's home. If you have the police looking around, then you are usually safe. The preferred front door is usually a manhole cover laid gently on a verge. If the police find this, then they are usually unwilling or unconcerned with lifting the cover assuming it is a water drain.

The real problem comes when the Highways Agency maintenance guys take a good look, and they realise that there is no need for a drain cover when there is no drain.

Most of the conversations that have been overheard have surmised that "it was probably kids building a den" and "I used to do that sort of thing when I was young".

With the lack of combined purpose, you are usually safe. The maintenance guys are not looking for a crime and the police are not looking for a drain, so somewhere in the middle the bankers tend to get by.

Food is a big problem. Bankers are not carrying out jungle warfare, nor do they automatically posses the skills to make nettle tea, mushroom medley etc. The ability to eat well is a skill and knowledge that is acquired over many months and years.

Roadkill is a big bonus. How many times have you passed a dead fox or bird on the way to work only to find that it has gone by the time of your return? Birds you say, other foxes? Bankers more like. A quick dash out of the undergrowth or putting on your Highways Agency fluorescent jacket for authority, often yields a take that can be used for at least two meals.

The kill should be fresh. You must have almost seen it happen to ensure that it can be cleaned and made good before you eat it. Although it would be fair to say that the bankers have a more resilient immune and digestive system, this doesn't make it bulletproof. The meat should be stripped, inspected cleaned and cooked in record time. No entrails are eaten, only pure meat, and the waste of the kill must be disposed of some distance from the bank.

The last thing you want is people seeing copious amounts of birds, foxes and other scavengers hanging around for the scraps. It won't take the authorities too long to suss out that something's happening. It's all about balance. You must take the breaks when they arise and concede to the bigger picture when things don't go your way. Everything is a bonus, and nothing is unfair.

It is well known that the average human can survive up to 10 days without food. Bankers found that they could stretch that a little but only with careful planning. The things that the bankers couldn't avoid was the cold and wet. If you chose to live out in the wild, then getting cold and wet in the Great British Isles comes with the territory. The cold was worse than the wet. If you get wet, then you always try and make sure that you have a spare dry set of clothes squirreled away. You then either hang the wet stuff out to try or you bite the bullet, keep your dry stuff for the night and then wear the wet stuff during the following day and use you own body heat to dry it out. Now there is no kidding that this is an emotional exercise, but it is a tried and tested method used by the armed forces.

The cold though is another matter. Once cold (and with minimal food for energy) you don't have very long at all before hypothermia sets in. You can bury yourself a little or create a wind break, but you must keep warm. The bankers generally found that by rotating bundles of moss or dried leaves it was possible to survive but in extremis there were times when he had to admit defeat and break into one of the roadside metal sheds which housed the temporary road signs just for some respite from the biting winds. God he sometimes missed carpet so much.

4

They hadn't started out together as a couple, although they took to the banks in this area for vaguely similar reasons and they had been drawn to each other essentially from the first meeting. They shared common dreams and perspectives and had learnt to trust each other very quickly. All bankers know that it is far easier to love someone way before you ever trust them. It's not about trust for monogamy, nor trust that the dinner will be ready or that the bins are put out. But a trust of protection, survival, integrity and sanctuary; will they hold that space for you when all you want to do is run?

They had both acknowledged that they hadn't become bankers to find love or a partner. So, they both needed to have the main purpose behind them being there as fundamental and overriding before anything else.

They would spend weeks and months apart, just banking. When they did come together, they would spend time holding each other and watching the fiasco of the roads unveil before them.

To them it was like watching ants on a mission. Just parading along, all in line, all with hypnotic preordained purpose. You don't necessarily know what the purpose is, nor do you ever truly question that purpose; you just do it and follow the rest believing that "following" is it.

They would laugh at the rest of us alright, but they also cried. They were envious, no, jealous to extreme some days. The liberties that those on the roads enjoyed smacked you right in the face.

The freedom to move and chose without fear. The ability to stand up and be counted. To work or leisure without real consequence was massive. But that was not banking. By making the choice to bank you gave up certain rights to those freedoms. The world and society had made its norms and there weren't really open to debate. The only way they could ever see of this happening was a pipe dream. Like an earth-shaking event. A world where all the infrastructure had disintegrated, and people were left to survive but in harmony. This they knew would never manifest itself. The moment this happened the human programme would kick in, the possession, the rules and regulation, the need to organise and control would quickly generate all that they hated.

Bankers knew that when you really looked at it, there wasn't a need for any of this. We are led to believe that you need a code or moral model to follow. Why? Would anarchy really reign? Would human wickedness truly see us eradicate ourselves? Probably not, but that would be asking far too much of the human race to consider. They are perhaps too far down the road of obedience to even try this as a concept let alone in practice.

They had discussed this issue many times, and now knew that banking was probably as close as you got to the ideal in a very small but significant way.

So, they lay back and talked. He would love to listen to her thoughts and dreams and she his. Talking was not essential, unless perhaps there was information to share about changes to roadways, verge control etc, but sometimes it was just nice to talk. They rarely spoke of their worlds before banking. Not that this was painful or full of bad memories, just that it held little in the way of interest. The only time they did speak about the time before was to recall experiences not instances. The experiences aspect was of benefit and interesting. The instances just served to ratify why they had turned to banking in the fist place.

When they were together, they had opted to use a large and densely planted bank just north of Clanfield on the A3. The A3 is a beautiful stretch of road (even by banker's standards). It winds gently through the north part of Portsmouth and on through the top part of Hampshire. Even though it ultimately crosses the M25 and through into London, it has had very little intrusion by the way of modification. The patch they had chosen obviously held a natural contour of the original area as there were still some old Roman ruins just to the east of their plot. Whilst the ruins may have offered more in the way of protection from the elements they chose to stick to the bank. Not due to some pious "true" way of living just that every now and again you would have either some curious historian poking around or some teens trying their first sexual fumbling or rolling joints. It was just much safer to stick to the bank and use the ruins as an addition.

Besides this, the bank had obviously been added to when the road was being developed and the ground was both relatively easy to dig and had a good drainage aspect.

The bank looked directly over the road for a good five miles northward and there were no visible or obvious reasons for anyone other than them to be there.

They had studied the bank for some time prior to deciding. They checked the visibility from all angles and even noted the aerial view. They checked for access, food, and clean water, and even where the nearest assistance phone was. Most importantly they had checked for several days on the potential for hold-ups or queues forming thus increasing their detection rate. Everything had to be in place to make this place right, even if they could smell something from the near by farm or lay-by, this meant that others in turn could smell them.

With the verge being heavily planted with elderflower and rhododendron with there was plenty of shelter from the wind and made it far easier to place the water collectors without being noticed.

Although the fires that were lit for cooking were usually at night, they had to be careful and sure that they could disperse the smoke through the bushes to avoid it being picked up in the headlights. This involves an intricate system of firstly burying the fire within the verge to hide the flames then hooking a fan and pulley system with wheel hubs to sweep the smoke over the crest. With caution this had worked very successfully. The only time a vigilant farmer had come to investigate, and the fire was out and hidden before he had stopped his Land Rover. Again, probably assuming that the smoke had stemmed from kids in the ruins, he left without note.

When she did move about, it was usually to the north. Sometimes as far as the M25 but usually more inland towards the Hants / Surrey border. This for her was ideal; she could use the surrounding farms for food and gave her some short respite from the noise of that bloody tarmac.

She would usually say that she was off, and he had learnt not to enquire or press too hard as to why. So long as she would let him know that it was her and not them that needed space then he was happy. He was much more a sedentary person and enjoyed being so close to his former home of Portsmouth yet being so desperately sad that he was so far from residence in it.

Besides, he chose banking for him not for them. He was in heaven just thinking and being as he was. She often felt that this limited his experience, but this was exactly where he wanted to be and where he wanted his experiences to be.

His favourite time was spent on the banks of the river Meon shortly before dusk. He had become a dab hand at tickling some of the wild brown trout and the sizable rainbows which managed to escape from the nearby fly fishery. He had even managed to tie himself a couple of very successful flies. Yes, this officially was stealing but it did fall within the rules of "stealing for survival only". Plus, he reckoned that what he had given back in terms of husbandry and bank management equated to a few fish every now and again.

His knowledge of wild berries and edible mushrooms had increased significantly when trading info with the other bankers. He was now seen and sourced as somewhat of an old hand and others newer on the path were often directed his way.

Now the most difficult encounter you will ever has a banker, is that with other bankers. How do you tell them apart from those on the outside?

Firstly, you can be confident that if someone managed to track you down then must know what they are looking for and where. Should this fail then their appearance usually gave them away. Not that they were dirty, it's just they looked slightly "earthlier" than the rest.

If none of these satisfied the criteria to identify you as a banker then a password, well more of a passphrase was used. The opening line from the one being approached would always start with "where are you going?" The reciprocal refrain would always begin with "not that far" Now although this may not be as abstract a response as you might imagine. It does serve its purpose. Let's face it if you met someone coming out of a hole in the side of an embankment in the middle of nowhere, and they asked you "where are you going" you probably wouldn't say "not that far". But and here comes the clever bit. If you overheard someone exchange these phrases, then you probably wouldn't take too much notice.

Anyway, it works and works well. Once pleasantries have been exchanged then the usual discourse on journeys, encounters, and "what's new" have taken place then the real learning begins. There are several fixed areas which must be discussed to ensure that all essential knowledge has been passed over. Both parties are expected to share their knowledge, no matter how limited on each area. First there is shelter and the construction of, then food and how to process it properly, next follows all the sundries like heat, water etc. Now by following this pattern religiously a mass of ideas and tried and tested methods have evolved which have led to banking being a sustainable way of life.

If you place into context that you may only ever meet two or three per year, then you can see how vital this dialogue really is.

This was exactly how they met; he had been banking for at least 15 years prior to her arrival, and she was just starting out following the dream and ideal. She had been tentatively adopted by a group of others who shared a more communal existence. They had taught her the rules and basics, but this wasn't really the kind of life she wanted to lead. She had dreamt of a much more nomadic and simple style without the confines of a group, bankers or not.

His passing through was just the excuse she needed to leave. As with bankers there are no hard feeling when someone leaves, nor any feelings of value placed upon the before or after. She was thankful to them but saw that teaming up with him was much closer to what she wanted.

He hadn't been looking for a companion, certainly not someone as new as her to his world. But according to the lifestyle he followed he accommodated her none the less. This accommodation quickly grew to be more, and probably more than either of them had wanted.

This wasn't a love story, rather the start of a very, very steep learning curve. He had taught and she had listened. Then, as her ability to manage as a banker grew, she found herself wanting more and more time apart from him. She adopted and immersed herself in the rubrics of this way of being and found this the place that she belonged, alone and not by his side. He used to love the sensation of human touch with her. Her skin was soft to touch, and she had certain innocence within her soul without being naïve. When the weather was warm enough, they used to make love in the early evening on an exposed grass mound not far from their bunker. Was this just sex? Quite possibly, but it never came to a conclusion as birth control was not something that was an option for them on the banks, so as he always told her, he got off at Fratton. (the second to last stop which didn't go all the way). For him at least, it was about a connection with another living, loving person, someone who truly 'got' him for who he was. For him this was Important; this wasn't about some cheap drunken fumbling's but rather a connectedness and sharing the ideas, hopes and aspirations of the soul.

Some two months after she left, he had been informed by others that she found that banking was not enough for her, and a real inner darkness has consumed her. He knew it was there, but he was never too sure if it was the darkness chasing her or her chasing the darkness? This wasn't a negative self-destruct act, rather that some souls cannot be contained by the light and shadows of this world, and that sometimes, just sometimes a soul belongs more completely to the entire universe and not just this planet. Cosmic, I guess!

She had thrown herself from a motorway bridge. What she lived by, she died by. He didn't think that she wanted to die, she just wanted the pain to stop or in her words "for the journey to go on"

Of course, he felt bad and more than a little bereaved, but he knew that she was not his to own nor his to feel sad about. He did however feel that she was selfish towards the driver and passenger; who were a newlywed couple whose bonnet she had slammed onto. Till their dying day they would be haunted by the memory of the anguished, terrifying look on her face at the point of impact and forever wondering if they could have done more to avoid her. Her pain had stopped alright, but her method had only served to pass this pain onto two other people who were totally innocent other than being in the wrong place at the wrong time. These were selfish thoughts though as he could affect no change for either party. He had heard of others who were in search of that nirvana and had felt captured or confined even by the world of banking. These people tended to lack the grounding or awareness of the human frailty. They tended not to accept that there were always going to be confines and limits and this was all part being human. You can't escape this; all you can do is to try stretching what this means to you as an individual and attempt to find a place or way this best fits your own mould.

5

He didn't move on; he didn't really need to. She had gone from the banks or given herself over to them.

Nothing had changed for him. Periodically others would pass through and offer those pregnant pauses of condolences when the incident came up in conversation. He was a banker not a mourner or lover or indeed partner, so he just went right back to banking.

He knew the great darkness himself. It wasn't acute for him, but he acknowledged that the darkness and light were there in equal measure. Just when things seemed to be going too well, the great cosmic dance would throw him a curve ball. It was a liminal state that had to be respected but not feared.

His time and energy were now being taken up by a far more serious matter than her suicide. After all that couldn't be changed.

He had just noted a temporary compound being erected a few miles north in a lay-by. This meant only one thing; road works, and road works meant only one thing, and that was people.

After the first few days he took the liberty of breaking into the porta-cabin for a closer look. Sure, enough there were the plans to widen the roads by three metres each side and the thinning of all adjacent verges.

This was always going to be an occupational hazard for the bankers, but an extreme annoyance just the same.

He had choices, he could either opt to pack up, cleanse the area and move on, or take the riskier option of trying to stay put throughout the works. The latter options held massive problems for him. He would have to literally go under ground for a period, his access and movement throughout the day would be practically nil and he didn't really know how long the works would take.

As with all maintenance, the workmen would usually work on three or four projects simultaneously, rather than complete the first then move on to the next. By doing this they would appear to their bosses and everyone else to be very busy in various locations. This would invariably extend the amount of time they had for each of the sections whilst having (at the end of it) completed three or four jobs. As this was an hourly rate job rather than a fixed price, they could make considerably more.

He needed to do both. He could not stay as he was, as the risk would have been too great and the conditions too hard, but he needed to be close enough to "liberate" some valuable items. First, he desperately needed a new hard hat and a new contractor's jacket. These were essential for those times when he had to cross over worlds. Then he needed to have access to the technical data detailing the workings of the new solar panels which were springing up everywhere. With this he could seriously advance the knowledge of the banking fraternity to power uploads of projects and processes, water purification, communication, etc

He had discussed this idea with other bankers and there was much contention as to the legitimacy of such an act. This knowledge and indeed the units themselves were not for survival in the strictest sense and for many seemed to bend the rules too far. He held a different view. He saw the liberation of both knowledge and equipment as taking the banking ethos to a new and more advanced level. After all, he argued that bankers did not sign up to living in the dark ages, rubbing sticks together for heat; and this was, in the grand scale of things, quite a simple principle.

Disagreements over such matters were very serious indeed. This potentially challenged the very constitution that the bankers relied on. He knew that. Keep doing what they have been doing and they would get left behind and exposed or keep pushing too hard for change and he would be considered a hypocrite; bending the rules too far ends up just replicating the world they had all left behind. And hence banking would become no more dimensionally different than anything else they had known. He also knew that going ahead with such a separatist act would alienate him from the rest and potentially cause a schism of massive proportions.

He knew the rules all right, he helped shape most of them, but he felt that banking had to move. It was an evolution not a retreat facility. The roads had changed; the infrastructure had changed; Why not banking? For sure the principles of collecting water and the attainment of food remained the same in principle, but for him that was not enough. With the advent of all the cameras, and surveillance it was becoming increasingly hard to move. This coupled with the ever-increasing birth of new business parks and commuter estates had led to a push pull situation of claustrophobic qualities.

He reasoned that that to obtain and use such technology would give back some of the freedom they had always enjoyed. By using the solar panels to monitor the cameras and Highways Agency movements would just be matching the outside at their own game. More a counter measure than retaliation.

This needed to be sorted out and soon. The reports of near-miss detections were growing. There were a few more cyber geeks being employed to watch those monitors day in, day out who were more concerned with the activities on the banks rather than the roads themselves. Part of this had been attributed to the increase in idiots chucking bricks off the motorway bridges, but the bankers felt that that there was an unhealthy interest being shown in certain quarters.

Short term, this wouldn't be a problem as there were positively thousands of miles that were at their disposal. But with the apparent zeal for "big brother" observation this was starting to generate certain no-go areas.

Time was on their side for now, as the UK Government with like everything else had a rolling programme and implementation phases, which were years behind schedule. Thank God they didn't ring fence the cash for the roads.

Tampering with any of the cameras or technology was a delicate matter. Too many incidents of faults or vandalism and this generated more interest, more people. But leaving them alone was equally hazardous. You see the new style cameras have an arc of vision far beyond that of the bankers. They can be swivelled and zoomed in to pick up very finite detail indeed, and you never know when passing by one whether it is live and being monitored or not.

The best time to pull the plug on them was directly after the cameras have been serviced or commissioned. As the Highways Agency, had chosen to sub-contract all the maintenance work they were based on raised orders. The first chap turns up, installs the camera. You follow very shortly after he has done his initial test and cross wire the circuit. This is then reported as a fault in the system. They then raise a separate order with a different contractor to investigate. He then turns up to find that the system has been cross-wired and refuses to sort the problem stating that it is a commissioning fault caused by the competition, and not a repair. This goes around and around and usually takes about two – three months before the camera is reinstalled.

Bingo. Out of complete disunity and piss-poor communication, you get yourself best part of another quarter of a year on the banks.

In the life on the verges, there is no one place or gathering where such issues are raised or agreed. There never has really been the need. Besides trying live in a world of separation and solace and freedom would be made completed null and void by some Grand Lodge meeting. To this end, everyone shared the same autonomy and parity to choose how and what they wanted. Ideas and changes had always just seeped round the banks like a crescendo, gently modifying the life in a very subtle way as they went.

Without the need for any kind of two thirds majority he had likened his idea to progress with the harnessing of the technology as a different branch rather than a fundamental change.

He noted the concerns of others but was adamant that if such a change in the cross over of the two worlds was bad, then this would be exposed and rejected by natural selection.

Should this alter his, and the ability of others to go on banking, or caused a resurgence in interference from outside then this would cease by necessity.

With the echoes of such a declaration filtering back, he was able to ascertain that this course of action would probably be acceptable on a small and singular effort.

Within a short period of time, he had managed strip down and re-wire two solar panels and lay his hands on a central control box with monitor. Although the reception from these was not great, he had managed to take a cloned image of everything that the control centre saw. Whilst this was fascinating at first, he found himself slip into the same trap as the outside world. He was spending vast amounts of time watching others on the roads like some reality TV programme. This realisation that he had deviated so far from that path of banking made him sick. Like a self-fulfilling prophecy, he had been absorbed all too easily.

From this point, he made a conscious effort not to watch any area of surveillance that was likely to be occupied by another banker.

Instead, he switched his attention as to how to use the power that was being generated to better the base processes they already had. Water was probably the easiest one to start with, so it wasn't too long before he had rigged up a portable element which was heated by the electricity. Collected rainwater was then passed over this in small quantities, then becoming steam. This was all housed under a metal wheel hub from an HGV. When the steam hit the cold hub, it would then condense back to water around the edges and produce all the water you needed minus the usual acid and debris.

Whilst fairly simple in construction this exercise was not without some sharp lessons in the basic of physics. Without the aid of a transformer, he had on many occasions become the earth for the element. This often-rude wake-up call just reinforced to him how reliant he used to be on "just" switching something on, "just" expecting something to work. And now this was about making it work for real and coming very close (perhaps too close) to some of the most powerful, yet natural forces on earth.

Whilst he was no engineer, he did posses a fair bit of technical knowledge on the rudimentary processes of science and technology and other crude, yet working devices soon followed. He was able to use an electric hot plate made from sheet metal for cooking on, and even developed a system whereby he could fake faults being detected in nearby areas on the emergency phones to distract any further attention to his patch.

But he had begun to struggle. He had found his whole existence being taken up with subversive actions to hide and confuse those on the outside. He had even noted that his mind set had changed. He was becoming obsessed with the concept of enemy and surveillance. This was making him tired, and the days upon days which he used to spend just thinking had drifted into endless moments and situations of panic and hiding. He was no longer free as he had been, he had now become trapped.

He had to change something, but not quite sure what. It wasn't just about getting rid of the new-found technology nor was it essentially moving away. The change that was needed had to come from within.

6

Banking had lost its purpose for him. He had been separated from the concept that used to be so simple yet so complete. He felt that he had been infected in some way by those on the outside without ever having directly met them. He reluctantly had to acknowledge that he had become the victim of his own relativism and reasoning. Squaring every circle by his own standards and thinking with little or reference to the history from which he had come from.

He knew he couldn't leave the banks but had to find a way out of this mess before he found himself doing exactly what she had done all those months ago. The long shadows of weight and oppression had started to fog his mind and he felt that his breath was being restricted ever tighter.

He noted that it had all started when he chose to leave the outside, and he had made a journey, both spiritual and physical to this place which he now called home. He needed to recapture the joy and how the outside had made him feel and what it was that was so good about banking.

He knew he had to return out there. He knew this could only be a temporary measure and that he could not tell anyone else, even as an experience exchange.

He thought long and hard, but even this was painful. Every time he suggested to himself that he should go, his own argument would come back. That is the problem with banking, you have no sounding board, you have no shared reasoning. From all of this he had found a peculiar sense or irony in the fact that the only place that could possibly make him whole again was exactly the place he come from with such desire and fervour.

He had decided he had to go back to find himself. He prepared what he could, although he had to nothing really to take back.

He ditched all the equipment he had accumulated but buried the essentials like his jacket and water purifier. These he would need on his return, and he knew, or hoped and prayed that there would be a return.

He cleansed the area he had been occupying and made good to the banks where he could. Even though he was returning he cared deeply about the verges.

At first light, he made his way two miles south to the nearest lay-by and waited.

Again, the irony of the whole thing came flooding right back when the van that pulled in to give him a lift displayed "Highways Agency" right across the side in a blazing logo.

The driver, happy to drop him in Portsmouth town centre was curious as to how he come to be standing on the side of the A3. But he seemed satisfied with the lie about a marital argument that got out of hand causing him to alight the car at such a strange place.

Once in the town centre it began very quickly. The strange sense of pressure and conformity that seemed to emanate form the very pavement below him. Even those just wandering down the road seemed to be following something intangible. Their purpose and destination seemed to be programmed and ordered.

He felt lost, and not least of all because he had given up all knowledge of how to act, how to behave, how things worked.

The very practical things he had left behind long ago had faded long past into the back of his mind; he certainly didn't have an address and was not sure whether he could even remember his National Insurance number. This didn't concern him too greatly as he didn't want to get that far back into things, he wasn't coming for employment or health care but only to find himself.

As with any main city the pace in the air started to pick up with alarming rate. This morning was no different. The buses had stared to arrive, and the volume of workers and school kids soon increased to a point where they began to change direction to avoid colliding with each other.

He instantly needed space. He began to panic. What was he doing? He had only been crossed over for one hour and already he found himself totally alienated and divorced from anything around him. This wasn't just rural verse urban life crisis. This was like another planet, another language and culture all together.

He moved quickly to Victoria Park just by the train station. He needed space and green things and he needed it now. Once there he sank, he sank in thought and posture. All he wanted to do was run to the nearest bush and hide. This is what he knew, and all he'd known for many years.

Victoria Park sits right in the heart of the town centre. It holds a couple of massive greenhouses and is flanked round its borders by flower beds, and it was and still is the much-needed oasis of calm and serenity in a mad, mad world.

Although it is central to the heart of town, it is surprisingly quiet. This may be due to the people who visit the park and their reason for being there. If you could place a bubble over the park for just one day to capture all the thoughts and dreams of all these people you could probably float the world. As with many other parks they tend to hold the best and worst of all that we are. The sad people use the parks for solace, the lovers for their laughter. The troubled for reason and the lonely for company.

It didn't take much for him to discern who was having trouble at home or work. Those who were in love and could not see the park for each other. Those who were lonely just wishing the time to pass. If only he could lift up the separate people in the park and transport them together, they would certainly be able to heal themselves.

The park is surprisingly well maintained though not in overstated way and it lends itself to be whatever the users require.

He now had to focus. He had come back for a reason, although not too sure what he was looking for, or where to find it. He had to concede to himself that he could not be part of this world without adopting at least some of its necessities.

He was going to need money. He thought about stealing it outright from some church or honesty box, but he didn't really want to take anything from this world that wasn't absolutely essential to his return.

He noted the number of people sat on the neighbouring benches who even in this day and age currently had little or no regard for their own bags or rucksacks. His attention to this seemed more acute than theirs. He wasn't too sure why. Maybe, like other criminals and petty thieves it was because that was his focus. Or maybe it was due in some part to the fact they were so busy thinking about the processes and demands of this world, and he had left all that behind many years ago.

He struggled again. He had not given up his conscience or his moral compass on leaving the banks and didn't want to add to the fears or pressures of anyone in this world. God knows they had enough of them, without him causing them more hurt.

He had no other option besides stealing than begging, so he settled for that. As he looked to choose his spot, he noted that several others were already laying claim to the prime spots. There was hierarchy between the other homeless fraternity, and this was even more noticeable when the "Big Issue" trader turned up.

The guy looked rugged, possibly of Baltic descent. He had the best pick, right outside the entrance to the Cascades shopping complex. Almost with some legitimacy and ritual he laid out his coat, settled down his dog and assumed the crossed legged, head down posture.

He would soon discover that this was not some act for the crowd, nor some marketing ploy, but it stemmed from a real sense of worthlessness and rejection. Even on the banks he had maintained his own personal esteem, but here (despite the noble cause of the magazine he was selling), these guys along with the rest, had lost all that meant to be human.

As he sat, the coins did start to roll in. Usually within a silent exchange, but sometimes the odd word of compassion.

It wasn't too long before he realized that he was offering a form of service. The passers by would approach looking very concerned and with heavy brow lines. Then once they had given the cash, they appeared to move on with a sense of great wellbeing. By giving him cash they had made themselves feel better. The more downbeat he looked the better they would feel. His position in life had made them feel grateful, almost affluent in their own right.

With this realisation, it eased his pain and humiliation to point of being bearable, that was until his frequent run-ins with the other beggars began. He could not reconcile how even those that passed him by without giving any money had managed to either look the other way or offer a smile of sympathy. But the other dwellers on the street, those in the same situation had become so twisted and resentful. Like he was potentially taking money that belonged by right to them.

7

Even if he didn't acknowledge them straight away, all these things were helping his cause. All the little incidents which caused him pain or insult or just thought stirring were making him recover. Like that of an alcoholic, his journey had begun one day at a time. He felt that he was beginning to recall and recognise why this world was so abhorrent, and why he had left it so long ago. There had been so many changes to the world in terms of technology and infrastructure, but all of this seemed to be a veneer. The inherent mistrust and greed had remained. The ability to commune with others and even share had continued to dwindle, but they seemed to live with, if not thrive off it.

His favourite author, Kerry Walters had noted that people saw God as represented by truth, beauty and goodness, and yet in our desire to be more god-like we are actually consuming truth, beauty and goodness. He saw this in city everywhere he looked. Everything had a *hook* or a price, everything seemed loaded with sinister undertones of greed and manipulation and conformity. Where was genuine altruism? Where was the love?

With enough money, he could feed himself adequately from the market by the Tricorn. Late afternoons were better when the traders would rather sell things on the cheap rather than cart them all back to their lockups.

Of an evening, he would saunter down to the harbour walls and watch the plethora of sea craft that would use the Solent. He mused over the thousand upon thousands of people who had passed through the harbour mouth, the Romans, the Venetians (perhaps they were akin to bankers on the sea?). He felt a sense of continuity with these people, and it did in some small way reconcile him to the rest of humanity. After all, if they had managed to survive and find a sense of harmony with one another then it did mean that human race (or at least this generation) was likely to survive, warts and all for some time to come.

He had made the mistake a couple of times of being out later than was safe around the pubs and clubs in the city. He could not help but think that the entire population must hold a real anger and real frustration within their own every day lives. Like a firework being touched by a flame. The people out for a "good night" were ignited by alcohol into pure rage. It didn't seem to matter who you were, if you weren't in their group then you were the enemy for that evening.

To him it fell nothing short of primeval warfare. This was not exclusive to the groups of lads; the groups of young women also seemed to be preoccupied with matching the blokes blow for blow.

The Burberry jackets and labels hanging like Christmas decorations seemed to typify a collective problem they had with their self esteem. If they didn't have the right gear, then this would be exploited by the rest. If the clothes were too poncy then this was wrong. If the clothes were too sedate, then this also led to alienation. This seemed to go further than just "fashion". The inability to master the right clothes and styles at the right time was akin to wearing the tribal markings of the opposition.

How interesting that people work so hard to get the money, to buy the clothes and other sundries that make you appealing, then to put yourself in a place with other like-minded people under the guise of fun or social recreation only to rear a beast like aggression that you know dwells within, with the sole purpose of hurting someone else. What quality, what refined people we had truly become.

His was not to argue, reason or indeed understand, he was here, for what he hoped to be a short time.

He would usually spend his nights sleeping in one of the parks within the confines of the city. Nowadays these parks do tend to afford some protection over an evening as they are locked by the City Rangers. Usually, the groups of kids who haunted these places are riding bikes so therefore tend to find alternatives, rather than scale the fences, bike and all.

He specifically chose the parks over some of the refuges or night hostels that were available. All too often they were overcrowded or full and just served to collect misfortunate people into yet another social group. Much like that of prisoners who are grouped together, then behave like prisoners and teach each other criminal things. So too do the homeless. When the only real conversation you have is with other people who society call damaged, and you are banded together for eating and sleeping. Then it is inevitable that something is going to wear off. His heart truly sank in these places; he knew what wealth and largess there was out there, and yet, the reluctance to share even a meagre amount with those in the shelter resulted in a Dickensian novel being replayed every day in the lives of these human beings.

He found himself surrounded by thousands of people throughout the day and yet he had never felt such a sense of extreme loneliness before. Even in the solitary world of banking he felt he shared a common theme with the others even though he may only meet them once a year and some never. But these people around him seemed to have no commonality, or certainly none that they were going to share with him. It was here that he found the starkest divide amongst people who shared the same postcode, same shops and moved inches from each other all day, and yet they had classed themselves without ever sharing a word. To those around him he had fallen off their ride or squandered the same inherited riches that they enjoyed, and he was not going to even share in their humanity. To them he was an oxygen thief.

Begging like banking affords you a huge amount of time to think. Even those who threw coins on his jacket didn't want to talk or taint themselves in some way. Whether it was fear of being drawn into helping a lost cause or just embarrassment of not knowing what to say they all stayed silent. This was fine to him. He in turn didn't want to get drawn into making them feel better about themselves by giving some huge lie about how he found himself at their feet. All he wanted was their cash and this was all they were prepared to offer.

His thinking whilst in the city had changed from that on the banks. Not just due to the environment, but all the hidden agendas and undercurrents that went with city life. The biggest difference was that whilst banking he had thoughts and concepts about how to make himself better in the eyes of his God. Whilst begging, all his thoughts seemed to evolve around how to make himself better in the eyes of others. The lucky breaks that he may have one day; the resentment about it was all someone else's fault that he was here.

He felt himself being swallowed up by all that he had run from, but this was good. He knew that by feeling this way and sharing that contempt of everything he saw and heard, he was on his way back.

Then it began.

After three months of the city, he had come to know who he was and what it is he wanted. There was no great flash of light, or myriad of voices calling him back. Just a gradual yet potent realisation that he was meant to be living once again on the verges, akin to a monk on holiday in Disneyworld.

He had started living this life and had been very successful at it, then he moved to the banks. Now he had come back and felt like one of the lowliest beings on earth. To this end he had known both the best and the worst of this spectrum yet in so many ways they were the same.

Whatever he did or tried to change in this world, he knew that inevitably he was a human being, belonging to this time and this class and that his efforts would be futile in a world such as this.

He had no doubt that they would survive and prosper in their terms and would make amends and efforts to better themselves and their conditions but for him this was not ever going to be enough. He needed to belong to a world where fundamental things could change. Where nobody held a rank or perspective that was superior to yours, just different.

The wretched way that he had been treated by other more fortunate people had just served to cement his belief that should their system and technology fail, then they would indeed be lost on their own planet.

When he grew tired of begging and had collected enough money for his food, he would often spend time looking for his God. Not so much in the churches or cathedrals that populated such a small island as Portsmouth with great regularity, but on the hill overlooking the city. Though the churches were cool and indeed offered a deep sense of sanctuary and peace, he could not quite divorce that feeling to be able to ascertain for certain whether it was the building and its imagery or a place where his God truly dwelt.

Whatever the reason, he always found a great sense of closeness to his deity whilst out in the open. He reasoned that should God ever care to be human again then he would certainly be a banker. From the hill God could see the world yet not have to be truly be part of it and he could affect its changes from a safe distance. Really, he knew that his understanding on this matter fell far short of what the

41

scholars would say is acceptable. But he had his faith and it kept him warm.

From the slopes of Portsdown Hill he could see the city moving about like it was a living hand. The roads seemed to be the veins and the islands dotted all around the fingers. The water surrounding the city ebbed and flowed as though the hand was opening and closing with supreme regularity. This really was a strong island.

The taste in his mouth grew more and more bitter. Such an inviting site, and such a cherished place to live, and yet he could never truly belong there again. The most perfect city and yet it didn't want him. At night he would watch the city glisten like a Christmas tree and yet this would always be the gift that was reluctant to give.

He spent a few days living in the caves that were hewn within the chalk pits. These were solemn places indeed. There is a maze of tunnels which are purported to stretch north through to Southwick, where the D-Day landings were arranged and south down to the dockyard. Most of this could just have been urban myth, but he wasn't going to take the risk to find out.

He'd always loved the face of the chalk pits, and often with a squint of the eye, he saw the rows of small gorse bushes that ran horizontally as a blank piece of sheet music. He'd tried on more than one occasion supplant the notes of his favourite piece onto the stave and to imagine the hill coming to life and singing to him. O glory, O light majestic, O city of ruin. O place of peace, whose hand ever tempts thee.

8

He was leaving the caves for his final stint within the city. He knew that he was almost at a point of return but had to go back for a little longer to truly purge himself of any delusions that he could or would want to return to their world.

When he woke this morning, he could smell and almost taste the wet chalk all around him. It had obviously been raining heavily as it had started to trickle within the cave. He had worked so hard to remain clean whilst staying on the hill and didn't want to return to the city looking any more pale or white than he felt. As he moved to descend the 40ft ridge that he was on, he felt it give. The bloody grip on these worn-out boots had finally held their last. He felt himself fall with such rush and force he knew he was in trouble. As he furiously tried to reach out for something to grab, he could feel the gorse bushes shred his hands. And then nothing.

When he came around, he could not move. He sensed he was still alive but couldn't quite work out why he felt such pressure all around him. Then he heard voices. They seemed to be far off at first, but then move very quickly into focus and clarity. By then he knew that he was still concussed and that he was lying strapped to a stretcher. This could not be happening. He had spent so many years being apart from people and just as he was planning his return it had gone horribly wrong.

He started to struggle, to break free from the restraints, but despite the words of comfort from the ambulance crew he knew that they would not let him get up and walk away from this one. He lay back with his face immersed in the fresh wet grass. He could hear the rain as it fell on the electricity pylons above. This crackle seemed to be the visible and physical song of something very powerful, which is usually unnoticeable.

As he gained an increased awareness, he noted that the paramedics were not alone. Just beyond the immediate area he caught site of the police keeping a small crowd at bay whilst he was treated. He could not believe that he had become so bloody selfish trying to find himself and was now at risk of exposing the entire world of banking. Question would be asked alright. Why was he up there? Where did he come from? Why wasn't he only any of the electoral rolls? Or databases?

As they lifted him into the ambulance he was blinded by the sun as it broke through the amid the showers. Although this was heavily clouded, he could see that it was very high, perhaps even noon. He reasoned he must have been there for some time before they found him. Later he would learn that one of a group of travellers staying on a nearby council field had stumbled across him literally (breaking one of his arms in the process) whilst out walking his greyhounds. This was of little concern now but getting out and free was.

Once transferred to the Queen Alexandra Hospital Accident & Emergency Department, he knew he would have to feign concussion or confusion to buy himself more time. This wasn't going to be too much of a problem as no one came near him for 25 minutes, and when they did it was only to check his vitals. He was aware that they were holding something back, and this became blatantly apparent, when the police officer and the duty psychiatrist swept into the room. When they had finished with their highly technical breakdown of his injuries (which resulted in nothing more than a broken arm, a few cuts to his head and a dislocated shoulder) they then began the probing real time.

What was he going to say? That he had lived on the verges and embankments for the past 20 plus years? He had then chosen to beg on the streets before going back to the banks. He thought not.

It was quite impressive really. They were both after different answers to different questions, giving little concern to what the other was saying. The officer wanted to know who he was and where he came from. Was he an immigrant to these parts? And why hadn't Big Brother gotten his number. The psychiatrist was more concerned as to what made him live in the caves and why he had thrown himself off the chalk pits.

Neither were going to get their answers today. With the mixture of morphine and anti-inflammatory drugs and a little bit of fine acting, he managed to feign a massive relapse into a drunken type of stupor.

As he was not able to answer any of their questions and as they were unable to locate a qualified social worker, they were not going to be able to section him under the Mental Health Act. This was possibly going to be the biggest break he would ever have.

It was whilst lying there that he had a nagging feeling. He was not too sure what it was, or even what it concerned, but he felt it every time the nurse came into the cubicle to check he was okay. Then it hit like a massive rush of blood to the head. She had touched him. This was the first time he had felt a compassionate touch in a very long time. He could not work out whether this was a truly heartfelt touch borne out of genuine concern, or just that she had done it for so long that it had become one the ways in which she plied her trade. Either way he relished every touch she made. Though not in a sexual way, it did make very part of his skin tingle like a giant erogenous zone.

With over stretched budgets and the absence of any detainment order he was left with the same level of supervision as all the other patients. This was regular, but not constant. He knew that to move when he had such a high profile within the emergency dept was not a good idea. He would have to wait until he was transferred up to one of the main wards. The nurses had informed him the police would still like to talk to him and would probably call in the next day or so.

Once he had been formally transferred onto the ward, and they had carried out all their usual observations, he was placed in a six bedded ward right outside the nurses' station. At first, he thought that such a move may falter his plans to leave, but as he watched he noted that the nurses spent more time flitting around the other wards on that floor and paid minimal attention to the main desk.

Fantastic. The obvious shortages within the National Health Service had only served to assist his cause once again.

He shared little in the way of verbal communication with either the nursing staff or the other patients within the room. He sensed that they felt unqualified to push him too hard on the how's and whys, rather leaving that can of worms to someone with a title. Amusingly enough he had told them that his name was Mr Banks and that he had not been in this part of the world for very long. If only they knew his concept of "not being in this world for very long", was so very fundamentally different to theirs.

Being somewhat a master of not being detected, he chose his time well. He had secreted his clothes in an unused communal room which was presently housing various mobility aids and redundant mattresses. This was directly opposite the patients' toilets.

Once the nursing team had completed their ward rounds for his room he moved quickly.

He muted to a couple of others that he was sneaking out for a sly cigarette. To this end he knew that they would at least join in the secrecy and smoke screen for slightly longer than usual, not wanting a fellow patient to incur that wrath of some of the more zealous and dictatorial staff.

He was mindful of the fall-out his disappearance would have on the nurses that had taken such good yet distant care of him. He had scribbled a note which detailed that he had chosen to discharge himself and exonerated both the nursing team and the NHS from all responsibility with regards to his current condition and any future consequence that this may hold.

He slipped the note onto the nurses' station as he passed through to the cubicle. After retrieving his clothes, he quickly dressed himself. The pain to his shoulder and arm was excruciating, but he kept focus on the task in hand. Once dressed he slipped out of the toilet and moved quickly along the corridor sticking to the walls. As he passed the visitors' waiting room, he grabbed an old paper which was lying on the table. He knew that to kill some of the boredom, other patients like him had become very aware of movement within the wards and especially different faces. He also knew that carrying even a paper under his arm would be a visual distraction for them to allow him to pass by without little attention.

This plan worked until he reached the stairwell. He had chosen to leave via the stairs rather than using the lift as everyone on the stairs was moving and usually in a hurry. Everyone that was, other than the two police officers chatting on the landing. He knew that one of them was the same one who tried to interview him before.

He panicked. He could feel his face explode as the blood rushed to very available cell and capillary. He couldn't turn around nor was there anything in that faceless chamber that would act as a distraction. He carried on with some pace praying that they would not turn or deviate from their conversation.

As he neared them, he could feel the paper slipping from under his arm. This was a disaster. He squeezed his elbow tighter and tighter; the pain was almost unbearable and had made his eyes start to water with what he could only imagine looked like a river down his cheeks.

He brushed by them as he went, only compounding the terror and pain that he now felt. For him though, God must

47

have been carrying him physically down the stairs. They did not stir from their conversation nor even turn with the contact that he had inadvertently made.

He moved quicker now down the rest of the flight he was on, trying to regain some element of composure, not so much for facial calm, more that he did not fall causing them to run to his aid.

Once outside the main reception he threw the paper into the nearest bin. Once again something which he used to his best defence, had nearly turned to be his complete downfall, and this was only a bloody newspaper.

He needed to distance himself from the grounds of the hospital and immerse himself somewhere busy. He had no money left so opted to bunk on a train at Cosham getting off at the main Commercial Rd station. Having been successful although in great pain due to the vibration of the carriage on the train, he moved quickly back to Victoria Park. He found himself on the same bench as when he joined *this world* some months previous. He was exhausted. Not so much from lack of sleep, more from the immense pressure that the last two days had caused him. Bankers no longer tend to possess the coping strategies that you must have for this world. He had gone for months and years with little or no pressure and certain minimal contact with other people unless that was on his terms.

Now he had found himself bombarded and cornered by what seemed to him to be thousands of eyes all fixed in his direction.

9

The attention and level of concentration was taking its toll on him, and he was low, very low.

It had rained constantly on and off for the last few days and he felt that his arm was becoming painful due to the cold and damp. He wearily made his way to the large ornamental greenhouses situated in the centre of the park. Although he had known of their existence for many years, he had never actually bothered to go in. Once inside the humidity was the first thing to hit him. A fine mist hung in air as the tropical palms and lilies canopied every available corner.

He was impressed at the hidden oasis that he had found within the bleak concrete mass of the city and knew why many bankers had previously worked for various parks departments. But he pondered over the question of why? Why would people dedicate so much of their time energy and money nurturing and caring for these plants? What is it that the plants could offer them, that they could not buy or replicate themselves? That was it. They cared for them as this was just one of a handful of things in their world, they could not buy. These giants were things of commitment and time, and were not open to mail order, or instant must-have commodities.

He was impressed, but then something gave these intentions (that were very genuine and pure) away.

Just in one corner he saw a wall mounted plinth bearing an award. And there it was. "The funding for this greenhouse was awarded by the council after receiving a distinction from the Royal Horticultural Society". His heart sank. He could now see that had the RHS not given this award then the greenhouse would probably have been torn down long ago. The council were keeping this going as a tool to further their own status. He knew that there was always going to be a trade off with such matters but try as might he could not find anything in their world that wasn't linked to some reward for someone.

Once back outside he wandered through the rain until he stopped at the fountain in the middle of the precinct. He was very much at a crossroads. He wanted to go home. He wanted to leave this place once and for all, but there something in the back of his mind that was saying he or they hadn't quite finished yet. He sat on the large flat lip of the fountain and reminisced. As a teen he had attended a nearby school, and they would often use the shopping precinct as a "playground" during their lunch break. Much to their amusement they would sometimes bring with them some of the god-awful lynx shower gel that all the lads used to get at Christmas. Quietly eating your Sandwich Spread or paste sandwiches the bottle of shower gel was discretely slipped from your bag and emptied into the fountain. Roughly 3 minutes later and the whole fountain had become a gigantic foam monster that spilled out of the fountain for several feet all around. Much chaos ensued, with office workers on their break running in every direction and small children squealing with delight, coupled with the sight of the local soap box preacher yelling about the end of time on earth unless you repent just made it all the more apocalyptic. They never could work out who had the control to turn the fountain off, but invariably they did and within minutes the foam behemoth was no more.

He caught the last bit of the rush hour begging by the mouth of the precinct which just about earned him enough for his tea from the market. He spent the night in one of the upper levels of the Tricorn car park. He remembered when there used to be a night club there, but now he could see why people had wanted to knock the thing down. The grey concrete walls had never even had a coat of paint, and the stalactites were creeping further and further down the eves. It was a cold and lonely place, although he couldn't help but think that even these barren walls held some kinds of echoes from the past. Like all the things they had seen and been party to had rubbed off in some way. Whatever he thought of them didn't matter now. They were his refuge from the wind and rain and that was enough for him as it had been for others in the past.

That night he was rudely awakened by a security guard doing his rounds. Although not unpleasant, the guard was obliged to move him on, or at least off his patch.

He had known this kind of antipathy before from the police. They didn't really care where you went so long as it was off their beat and out of the sight of everyone else. From this he began to understand why the homeless had been branded a silent or forgotten people.

He moved along to the warm air vents at the rear of the new shopping centre and tried to sleep with his arm on the ledge.

By first light he was already awake and in great pain. He took the last of his prescribed drugs and made his way to the toilets by the civic offices to make himself as clean as possible. This was an even harder problem for him than when he was living on the banks. The grime and filth seemed to impregnate every pore with amazing speed.

He could see why the mortality rate was higher in the homeless of the city than that of the banks. Although the bankers had a big problem with the fumes and pollution from the cars, they did at least have the respite of the air movement, and foliage all around. Within the city there seemed to be staleness which held everything in suspense even on the windiest of days.

He watched how the council sub-contractors spray cleaned the dirt and chewing gum off the pavement just inside the guildhall square and thought how he would love to be that slab. To be made clean, made whole again. If only he could go back and have a few of the layers which now haunted him removed, he would certainly have the last 72 hours washed away.

As it was still early, he found that he enough money for a bagel and coffee sitting outside a near by café. As with all meals he knew to eat slowly savouring every mouthful. The bonus with taking your time was that you didn't notice how early it still was, and every moment spent being almost normal, was another moment when you weren't sat on the floor begging. It was not about trying to forget, but more about trying not to remember. For a few short moments he had almost adopted the posture and presence of any other person in their world. Just by sitting at the table he had regained some small element of feeling that it was okay to hold his head up, okay to hold eye contact with people. Even though he knew that this was a temporary moment in his days it felt good to be counted again.

As he roused from his thoughts, he knew that the time was fast approaching when he would have to raise his physical and mental game again and return to the streets.

It was moments like these when he knew that if had the choice, he would opt to terminate his pathetic existence in this place and continue the path without the shackles of either his world or theirs. Being a banker was part of that process without ever making that final decision to take his own life. Now he wondered if he could still call himself a banker.

He did not cry too often, as there had rarely been the cause or need, but now he cried. He could feel the tears plunge downs his cheeks tickling his stubble as they went. He tried to compose himself but to no avail. He could do nothing but weep, and he wept from his heart. He was not just weeping for himself or his own circumstances, but for the very world that allowed and forced him to be without love or grace.

He could see that he had drawn the attention of both the owner and a couple of other people in the café. He could tell that despite their awkwardness, they would soon feel compelled to make an enquiry. As he left the table, he felt a sense of apology to them. They did not know him; they were not blame for his circumstances anymore than he was. But he had left them with a great sense of concern and had somehow saddened their day without even saying a word.

For the next couple of days, he followed the same pattern of begging, eating, and surviving. Whatever he thought he might be waiting for was just not coming in the way he had expected.

His arm began to heal and the abrasions on the side of his face were looking less and less unsightly. He just wanted to forget the whole incident which had nearly cost him and all the bankers so dearly.

Whilst passing the TV shops in the precinct he had realised that had probably missed out on many earth changing events over the course of the years of being on the banks. He sometimes sensed that his curiosity might get the better of him as he had toyed with the idea of sitting in the central library in front of the micromesh and scouring over all the backdated news stories. This would not serve him well. He had managed to survive quiet nicely without this plague of bad news being fed to him day in and day out, although he did reckon that by the laws of averages that he would also have missed out on so many good things that may have happened.

Before he had become a banker, he, like many others had held a long-standing passion for football. He often wandered how his boyhood team (Portsmouth FC) were doing. From the banks he used to watch the reams of away supporters' traffic their way down the motorway, trying to note on their return their level of animation or disappointment. When he first started doing this, he could tell what division they were playing in. But within a few seasons of team movement, he had lost all reckoning of how well or poorly things were going.

Along with football his other passion centred around the idea that he would one day develop a perpetual motion machine (PM). He had studied all the relevant definitions of what constitutes perpetual motion, and how the scholars and scientists had become very sensitive and pious to different variations. He kept his ideas simple, and this ultimately was his biggest mistake.

Unbeknown to him, the work he had been doing before he became a banker was being very closely watched. He had tried and recorded on his computer two very simple yet potent methods of realising perpetual motion. The first relied on the use of water filled canisters rotating on a wheel with different weights and spaces. After an initial push this would cause the wheel not only to spin but also gather a huge amount of momentum. With this being harnessed via a drive belt the extra speed absorbed the friction being caused by the moving parts.

This idea was unstable to say the least and whilst it flagged many of the basic rules of PM needed much more work to refine its potential to gain profitable energy at little cost.

His second and most advanced idea, Polarity Altering Machine (PAM, which also happened to have been his mother's name) was to use a circle of magnets fixed on a wheel with all the polarity facing the same way. This was rotating another magnet held centrally with a shield on the middle. By doing this and creating this shield, the positive polarity of the rotating magnets only saw the corresponding window of the fixed magnet for a split second. Then it would pass the second window seeing the negative polarity for the same amount of time. This caused the push /pull effect which made the cylinder not only turn but increase in speed.

Unlike the water idea, this was easier to harness and manage and relied less on other equipment which caused friction.

When he left his research, he thought of ideas as a "work in progress" with potential, but not much more. This work had fascinated him and was one of things that he sorely missed. That and his beloved workshop in which he had spent so many hours. To him this was his little piece of heaven. He had his tools, his music and his freedom to try new things without interruption. All this however it did not hold enough of an appeal or attraction as to stop him leaving to be a banker.

For him the notion of a layman's pipe dream was true, but for those who had found, tracked, and tried to replicate his PM ideas, they held massive interest.

He had only ever put saved sketchy and incomplete notes on his computer. He did this on purpose, as even back then he felt slightly uneasy about sending info to a place that he could not see.

It was quite early when he awoke in Victoria Park. He had begun to work out the Park Ranger's pattern for sweeping the park at the end of the day and successfully managed to find a small hole in the fence which divided the park from the railway embankment. Here he had made a temporary shelter using corrugated metal. The only downside to this was that he had be in the park before they closed the large metal gates, and somehow emerge in the morning without detection.

As he roused from his broken sleep, he felt that something was different. It had drizzled at some point during the night and this had led to a shallow mist forming right across the park. With this haze also came an eerie sense of peace and stillness. But something still wasn't right. He didn't know if this was an interior or exterior thing, but what he did know, that whatever it was it was affecting him in a profound way. His eyes started to play tricks on him; he was aware of strange yet beautiful dancing colours on the periphery of his vision. He closed his eyes in the hope that they would be disappear, but they were still there in the blackness of his mind. Beautiful, magical dancing colours. Entrancing yes, but they shouldn't be there. As he opened his eyes again the view of the park in the early morning was being bathed in these wonderous lights, as though looking through a kaleidoscope with reality being only a background to this newfound filter.

Then, as if a hydrogen bomb had been placed inside of him, he threw up. This wasn't a "being sick" kind of throw up, or a little puke this was a torrent of spew that that erupted from deep within with such velocity it literally emptied him from the inside out. Bent over, he was still aware of the wonderous array of colours in his mind's eye but then it started to darken very quickly, and he could feel that his ability to have positive control over his body was fading fast. His last sense was that he was falling; but falling into what and why?

10

It struck him like a sword running right through him. The news that King Arthur had fallen to Mordred. He had only been at his side in the Great Hall some weeks before. The very thought that all that Arthur had been, was now swallowed up and taken away filled the air with dread.

Although the hamlets and villages were small, the terrible news ran the land with great ferocity.

The panic that would last a generation had now gripped all the people throughout the kingdom. In an instant their everyday tasks had taken on a sombre meaning. The harvest now seemed worthless and the grazing without purpose.

All he could do was swallow. As the realisation of what he had been told started to sink in, he could sense the feeling of great emptiness consume him. Although dazed he could almost tangibly touch the ever-growing void which was spreading one by one as the other dwellers heard.

That evening he returned to his wooden lean-to within the forest basin. He and the others who shared his need for exclusion sat bewildered round the fire.

They had spent so many evenings with the King sitting round this very fire, talking, and sharing ideas about the charge they had been given. Now there was nothing. There was no one to lead them, no one to champion their quest (albeit secret) within the courts of his realm.

The forest darkened as usual, although this evening the blackness became even denser, as if it was being cloaked by some sinister undercurrent. The owls and other nocturnal members of the forest's eco system moved about totally unaware and unaffected by the King's fall.

Arthur had made himself available to the clan the moment he had known of their existence. He noted that even he as King was responsible to and for them, even if the path they followed differed from the rest of his subjects. He talked openly about a sense of jealousy. Not envy due to the restraints of his royal command, nor jealousy of their seemingly "free" lifestyle. He was truly at home with them and shared their ability to express and live through the ideals he also shared.

Their introduction to Arthur had been one of a baptism of fire. It was whilst he and other members of the group were being arrested by for treason and trespass (for living in a forest!!). Arthur himself had ridden past with his huge entourage. Thinking that he would wish to impress his fellow cronies, they felt that their days would be numbered to one at best whilst they were being hung or burnt.

To their surprise the King saw through their meagre and rather pathetic appearance and began to question the arresting soldiers as to the crime for which they had committed.

Finding only bravado and unfulfilled power in the claims, he ordered that they be released.

On his dismount it was evident that the rumours and myths surrounding Arthur's greatness held some degree of truth. Even with his full upper body armour, he was truly a great and powerful man. Arthur was one of those people whose charism shone through long before he opened his mouth. He was no manager or organiser; in fact, he had developed leadership into *followship* and the absolute trust and respect that his people had for him was evident every time his name was mentioned, let alone when he physically appeared. His long hair was perhaps the only thing shielding the true breadth of his shoulders. The King spoke in wise and gentle terms asking of his and the group's reason for residing in the forest. He seemed to be able to differentiate in mental terms, that they were unlike any other of the outcast who live and steal in his forest. He ordered his companions to dismount and take rest at some distance as he lowered himself before them to sit on a fallen oak.

He listened with courteous, yet intent enthusiasm as to their creed, nodding frequently to the ideals that they desired. He noted their honesty when talking about how they trapped food, but also their ability in some way to become custodians of the woods for his benefit.

With the King's assurance that they would share his grace and favour over them remaining in the forest, he left assuring them that he would return.

From this meeting he and the rest of the group moved deeper into the forest. It was not that they doubted the King's word, or that this should be some kind of entrapment. After all, had he wanted to, Arthur could have had them all slain by the arrow on the spot? They needed to move back into the forest to be able to reinstate what they were about, both individually and as a collective.

Neither he, nor the group would see or hear from Arthur for many months to come but this was not a singular encounter. They made their way further into the woods, and more importantly further away from the surrounding hamlets. They knew that their being in this place was a vocational response to a calling but could not align where this call had come from. Individually they knew that purpose and ultimate destiny lay somewhere deep within the realm, and this was shared in a sense of enlightenment every time their numbers grew.

The dense forest covered most of the land as far as they cared to travel. With the abundance of a truly natural resource such as this, life was relatively easy. He learnt much from the others in the group and had become quite a prolific resource on remedies and medicines extracted from the forest floor.

Knowledge such as this had not only supported the group when illness occurred but had in fact developed to such a stage where he and the rest of the group enjoyed an enriched health far superior to those folk living in the towns and hamlets. His ability to take a piece of bark or the root of a plant and concentrate it to such a level that it would provide a complete defence, was invaluable.

Within the forest basin they had a free reign on where to dwell. They would usually opt for a spot within easy reach of a stream. Not only did this provide clean water for washing and drinking, but it also meant that they never had to move too far for food. Fish were a plenty and deer needed to drink.

For those that knew of their existence within the forest they were considered to either be brave or possessed. Colloquial talk of evil spirits roaming the forest was commonplace. Talk of satanic rituals and demons seemed to preoccupy all tales being passed throughout the generations warning all children alike as the sun dropped on yet another evening.

To them this was ideal. Where others feared to tread it afforded them much freedom, solace, and security. They saw the woodland as their best companion not a place to be feared. Most of the substance behind these tales lay in the extreme quiet which consumed the undergrowth. From this, anything that made a noise and was not visible to the nervous was sinister and unholy.

The group were of great learning, and indeed derived from some of the finest family lines in the land. To this end they were knowledgeable enough to know that most of the mass hysteria behind the forest had derived from the Holy church and monastic orders. The church needed to manifest and identify the devil in some way, and the blackness and hostility of a forest in the Northern hemisphere served this purpose well.

On the inside they knew only peace, harmony, and co-existence with everything. They said their mass alright and gave thanks to God for everything, but this formula had stemmed from an informed awareness that the Satan lay within the towns, castles and hamlets themselves rather than in the wood. Indeed, it was apparent to even the less noble that the devil's work took place within the hearts and minds of men, rather than within lonely woodland.

11

His woodland lay just north of the Tor at Glastonbury and the main abbey stronghold just further south of that.

There was something about Glastonbury and indeed the whole west coast region. He was not too sure whether this was *something* that truly existed either within him or the land, or whether it was a subconscious and suggestive emotion that hung in the air due to all the peripheral aspects of the town.

The place was choked with "holies" and monastics, and for these he held little regard. It was not too many years passed when he himself felt called to answer his vocation and joined the abbey. The time at his abbey was truly beautiful. Once past the rigours of aspirant and novice training, he found a way of life in which he could be so holy and yet so worldly.

Once his work was over for the day, he would often sneak away to the far side of the abbey gardens and take rest in the orchard. From here he felt that his path was to bring God to His people and his people to God.

The sun would often gently slip below the flint abbey wall before he would concede to the cloister bell and sprint back for matins.

It was probably during this time that he was happiest in his life, yet this was not to last. From what he thought and found to be the happiest and most successful time in monastic and vocational terms was to ultimately lead to his downfall within the order, and expose the fallibility of both himself and others

It was at this time that a great charge of energy swept through the land. There was much talk and excitement over the announcement that had stemmed from the royal court. Arthur had let it be known that there was indeed a grail and a holy one no less to be found. There had always been this myth which had led many a greedy man to a lonely path.

Now Arthur was adamant that the grail was there, and he / we had been charged to find it.

Instantly the fat, wealthy and greedy mobilised themselves to Arthur's side. It was clear that this was not about some spiritual find for the good of the mother church or people of the land. Those that mounted first were there just to be seen by and with Arthur for their own gain.

Those in courts would huddle in secret chambers trying to suggest that finding this grail was indeed their own destiny. The young men who roamed the villages with such bravado managed to stir themselves into such frenzy, then off they would go before realising that they had no idea of what they were looking for, nor any idea of where to find it.

The effect of such mass hysteria was initially a good thing. It appeared to give all the peoples of the land young or old, male, or female a sense of purpose. However, it was not too long before it was evident that this had led a large number to think of the search as less about a fun waste of time, and more about an insular, consuming hunt for the Devil's gold. Whenever the grail was mentioned there was a sinister hush. Any knowledge which they thought they had was closely guarded. Each thinking that they were indeed closer and more deserved than the next.

The consequence of this was a much reduce attendance at mass. The people seemed happier to be out hunting for something that they wanted to believe in, with all its riches and fame rather than sitting blindly at a mass said exclusively by the clergy and in Latin. No, they had found a search and in their own tongue.

This national obsession coupled with the vicious hunt for Pelagian heretics had made the church and his part of the land a very unpleasant place to be.

Pelagianism had begun to very quietly challenge and enlighten the ordered thinking and belief system adopted by the people of the kingdom, albeit by a proxy vote! It had gathered much support to the idea that man was not carrying an inherent sin, nor was his salvation some way preordained irrespective of his own efforts for redemption. They had preached a licence of free will with the consequences very clearly laid out for the here, and the hereafter.

He had decided to break with the tried and tested method of witness and instead felt that he and ultimately God would be better served if he took the sacraments (that belonged to the people) to meet the people where they were, and in a manner that they wanted and could at least understand. For him, this really was acting as a conduit of grace.

He had not reckoned on the total and utter abhorrence to such an idea. He had outlined his proposed idea to the abbot in such a way as to give him some ownership and credit, yet the abbot would not even consider the slightest deviation from the rubrics.

All he wanted to try was to be able to spend some time each day outside the abbey walls and share their skills with the laymen and poor of the neighbouring villages. He was not talking change; he was muting at expansion in a way that they all profess every day with such piety. It appeared that even his enthusiasm and ability to champion this matter only served to anger the abbot further still.

This notion and plan was viewed by the abbot and many of the rest of the order as a matter of supreme disobedience and disloyalty. From this moment on his days in the abbey were numbered. First, he found that his duties had now been restricted by the house master to internal grounds work only. This usually meant working in the great hall or the kitchen. He could sense that every time his eyes strayed too far from the task in hand, they were met by those of another monk eyeing curiously and with a sense of suspicion in his direction.

Others would no longer be seen with him and this hurt him badly. The pain he felt from being ostracised so completely made him feel physically sick. He could not rationalise that these people around had called him "brother" for so many years. They had been in every sense his family and now nothing.

He would have understood better had his crime been to steal from the chancel purse, or even to speak of other unions or theologies, but it wasn't. His great err had been to think clearly and catch a small glimpse of what God really wanted. Surely their God didn't want his people to be carrying around this "sin"? nor would he want those he had chosen to store up their most precious gift of compassion and teaching and hide away at a time when his people needed them most.

He felt in some small way that this was the abbot's way of being able to boast they he too had encountered and eradicated a Pelagian heretic right from within his own order. This would surely impress the special envoy from Rome

The abbot called for him late that afternoon. The other brothers were readying themselves for evensong. The abbot spoke of individual and collective journeys, and how it had become apparent that his path would not be parallel or conducive with the rest of the order. He noted that since there had been "questions" over matters of faith that a time spent apart for reflection would be in his best interest.

It was almost laughable. He had never known of anyone ever returning from one of these "time for reflection" journeys. He wondered if he would leave the abbey and find a whole bunch of redundant monks just reflecting quietly somewhere! He thought not.

As he was ushered through the grounds to his cell, he could sense that they wanted his departure to be a discrete matter so as not to cause unrest amongst the other brothers. By this he was not troubled, he had just started to feel the immense and gut-wrenching darkness fall upon his life. As he left the hazy shadows of the inner wall, he realised that this would probably be the very last time he would see or smell the abbey again. He had known nothing else for such a long time that he almost forgotten how to behave outside these walls.

He was alone and frightened as the huge oak doors closed loudly behind him. It was as if they were signalling to the rest of the town square that another pathetic soul who had fallen from *their* grace was being booted out.

He could not reason the speed in which his fall had taken place, he could hardly catch his breath yet alone reason as to how or why God had allowed this to happen to him.

12

He ran quickly through the small town trying to avoid any attention, whilst being aware that a monk running through the tiny alleys at this time of night was hardly usual.

As he plunged his head into his hands, he sat heavily on the edge of wall surrounding the chalice well compound. Legend has it that the waters of the well sprung forth at the command of Joseph of Arimathea. As he looked into the water, he could only weep quietly to himself in pure selfish pity. With such hatred and vigour, he had been singled out as an example and now his purpose in life had become null and void.

He moved himself into the dense undergrowth that surround the bottom of the Tor and sought for some mental relief at least. This refuge that he so desperately required was to be that night, as he heard the bells from the abbey signalling the start of night prayer. He thought as to how many times he had listened and indeed tolled those bells from the inside. Now with every ring it seemed to pierce him deeper still.

Within a few days he had quickly realised that the staring and whispering from those around him was due to a reverent apprehension rather than with sinister intent. He also saw that his black hessian cassock enabled him to move, feed and speak with relative ease, which was of some comfort although he did feel that in some way, he was "cheating" these people, but his needs at this time was a must.

From that time, he had grown stronger each day constructing more sense for himself surrounding the events of those last few days within the abbey. This was for his own comfort and a very real necessity to develop some sense of self-belief and worth. He had to in some small way tell himself that he was not a truly godless and worthless being, his soul was worth saving and they in their turn were also to blame for his leaving.

He often toyed with an arrogant thought that God had perhaps saved him from the abbey to do his work, rather than saving the abbey from him.

Being back with the group, sharing a meal he left the thoughts that haunted him of the abbey far behind. He now shared company which although constituted its own kind of order, was bound truly by a bond that could not be tangibly traced or sourced to anything other than belief.

They would often question themselves as to what had brought them together and more importantly what sustained them. The life was often hard and the battle just to survive was always in your face.

They were somehow inextricably bound by some presence or mystical agenda over which they had no control.

It was late afternoon, and the sun was just gently tipping over the tips of the trees. There was a great sense of laboured stillness within the forest, the only things that were on the move was the occasional deer and the ever-present gnats swarming around nothing.

One of the group had returned from an over night trek to the nearest village. They had received word via the safe house that Arthur wished to meet with them once again the following day. This news was not only met with a sense of excitement and euphoria, but also a realisation that in some way this meeting was not just a noble or kind visit from the King, but a strange fulfilment of their very being together and future.

They readied themselves like warriors to the call. The place was made good and a neutral venue away from their camp was found. Although they had this sense of something predestined and virtuous, they could take no chances with securing the immediate vicinity.

A small number waited for Arthur at the mouth of the forest just by the open meadow. The rest held position around a very small enclosure looking much like miniature amphitheatre. They had their weapons to the ready and their swords honed to the cut.

To their amazement Arthur was only attended to by one small looking sage, who was positively dwarfed by Arthur and his horse.

The king followed cautiously yet willingly behind the band that had come to receive him, acknowledging their need for surety and secrecy.

As the group finally assembled the sun was still rising and the dew formed a soft mist in the backdrop of their vision. Two members were perched precariously on the flanks of the meeting casting a sporadic yet careful eye for unwelcome interruptions.

Whilst it was obvious that the King was indeed a noble and learned man, he wasted no time outlining his reason for the meeting. He spoke of the ever-increasing tensions within the boundaries of his home and kingdom, and his increased need for someone or some people that he could trust without the taint of human want and greed.

Arthur explained that whilst he was indeed the King of all the land and could have whatever his pleasure be, he felt a great sense of being trapped within his own life. He could not count too many of those around him as his friends or indeed allies. He would sort this situation out at a later date noting that it was better to have his friends close but his enemies, closer.

Arthur had known for some time that the oral tradition surrounding the grail had held more than a degree of truth. He had originally decided to put this in the public domain to generate massive interest and more importantly, to create the effect which was now evident for all to see. Every man, woman and child preoccupied and almost possessed by the interpretation of the grail being gold and bejewelled, sent straight from heaven itself.

The group and indeed Arthur, couldn't help but laugh despairingly as mental pictures flashed through all their minds.

The group were somewhat perplexed and confused as to why their King would knowingly mislead such foolish minds in what could only be described as a cruel manner. Arthur explained that whilst his deception was cruel it wasn't without purpose, and indeed this did offer some entertainment and pastime to largely otherwise simple creatures.

His smoke screen had been devised and implemented to shield and protect the real grail. Arthur's voice took a more serious and concerned tone as he emphasised that the only other living soul who shared the knowledge, he was about to impart was his own son Mordred.

The grail was neither a chalice nor a set of cruets nor indeed anything could that man touch. The grail was a secret whose design lay in the hearts and minds of some chosen men and women. When this formula was revealed through the work and sacrifice of these men, then the world would know how to live in a harmony far out passing any sense of peace we now held. Humanity would no longer feel the need possess the things belonging to another, nor place himself above the wealth or rank of his neighbour, instead its creed and desire would be truth, beauty and goodness.

13

There was a strange yet almost warm feeling amongst the group. Arthur sensed this also and beamed knowingly around the circle. He knew in his heart that the men in front of him were the cornerstone of a mission that could potentially unity the whole world.

The minds of the men ran wild with questions of when and how and ifs. They too were held by the same feeling of unity and the knowledge that their collective identity which much stronger than its parts.

As each one glanced at another they could already start to glimpse the role each of them would play with their different skills and attributes.

Arthur knew that this message was not a complete oracle on what was to happen and when. He would need to leave and seek for the discernment required, as to what was going to be needed next in this quest.

He had done the most important part by establishing that these men were the ones who were going to change the world by God's decree.

Once Arthur had left, he called the group to order. They needed to be grounded in some way to re-establish the most beautiful and pure thing that formed them in the first place. He suggested that wine and song be replaced this night by serious thought and contemplation. This was not necessarily to quell any specific thoughts, but to focus the minds beyond the fame.

He explained that by his own reasoning Arthur had not indicated that they be off on some foreign travel nor where their numbers going to grow or become renowned. The enlightened source that the king had spoken of could be literarily right below their noses. Without this further insight as promised by the king they would be better served by postponing all thoughts of grandeur whilst taking heart in the fact that they had indeed been called in a special and considered way.

The group retired that evening to the branch shelters that had been hurriedly wound before dark. As the darkness settled in there was very little sleep to be had, each trying to recall exactly what the great King had said and what the impact of his words would be?

If he truly meant that this paltry group of men could and should be the ones to throw open this secret, then this would be bigger and beyond that of any idea known before. Bigger than the church, bigger than the Romans, bigger still than life itself. With each thought came several others racing along behind. As each man lay in the complete stillness of the woods their very thoughts were almost shouting into the night.

Once the initial excitement had settled in then came the enormity and profundity that something like this held.

They were due to meet King Arthur two days later by the Eastbury pond just outside Glastonbury. They had set off the night before and rose early to make their way to the rendezvous. It must have been about just after 4am when the first light broke. You could tell that it was going to be a warm day as the mayfly were already getting busy taking flight. Occasionally the surface of the water rippled as a fish woke from its slumber to chance for an early bite. The haze gently rose from the pond as if mother nature was airing her sheet. It was still, it was magical it was a time to savour.

As the moments trickled into hours the atmosphere amongst the men gently shifted from enjoyment to patience to slight impatience. There was no time set and everyone knew that the stuff of life got in the way, but the King had never normally been this late and there was no sign from any of his men or "runners".

Shortly before dusk there was a terrible commotion coming from the south side of the pond. He was first to hear this and dispatched some his men to quietly skirmish round to from east and west to see what was going on. In an instance his men had located and bound a man bloodied from head to toe. His face was slashed on one side, and he was bleeding profusely from a shoulder wound. They brought him to the bank where the rest were waiting, and once he had established that the man was a friend of the group, the King he had him untied. Horror in a person's face is instantly recognisable. You can sense that they are trying to make sense of an unimaginable truth that they have seen and yet their mind is holding all things in suspense so as not to allow this horror to become a reality. He sat him down and had one of his men attempt to dress his wounds. After a few moments he began to speak. He was rambling about the chaos the betrayal, the madness. The man was clearly in shock but once calmed and dressed he began to make more sense. He explained how there had been a battle at Camlann. It was quite unexpected, but it quickly grew out of hand, Mordred had wanted something all for himself and would stop at nothing or no one to get his prize. Mordred had called out the King to relinquish to the truth or die. The battle had been brief, but ferocious with such a rage as he'd never seen before. The King had reluctantly but mortally injured Mordred, but youth was not on his side and before anyone could make sense of this madness Mordred had thrust his sword into the King's heart. Those who witnessed this were in disbelief, for as the King turned with the blade still piercing his very soul, he had an almost serene and gentle look on his face. He fell to the ground slumped across the body of his son and as one had given birth and life to the other, so now both lay in the squalid mud breathing their last. In that liminal state, there was love and hate, generosity and greed, beauty and evil. For every good thing in those two souls writhing around in the filth there was an equal amount of twisted hatefulness and here now as the story and history played out for all to see their life left them.

As the man continued to recall the terrible events of the day his mind began to wonder from the present, to what next?

If Arthur had been true to his word, then the only people who knew what this great mission was were now dead on a hillside. What then for him and his men? Was there an extension to this? Would they now take up arms for their beloved King to try and find out this truth for themselves?

Would there indeed be a kingdom anymore and who was next in line to the throne?

Later that evening his men gently gathered around him looking for that direction. They had already given so much and obviously were prepared to give him and the cause more, should he only say the word.

As he spoke, he knew the poignancy of his words as they were formed and left his mouth. There was to be no more cause. There was to be no more search for the grail or any such thing. Whatever this thing of goodness and truth had been it also had the capacity to become a cancerous yet alluring spot in the hearts and minds of people.

He reconciled that if this was indeed a thing of God and it was God's will that this thing should be gifted right now at this time in history, then it was also in God's providence to remove this chalice or curse until a time when humanity could be trusted with it in the future.

They had answered the call of God and King and were found ready and waiting for service and yet at this time it had not been called upon. Their job was to now carry on waiting and watching for the signs and times when that call would come again, if ever.

Following the events of that evening, the group stayed in the local area for a few more days before gradually moving east back into the forest and hedgerows from whence they came.

Little or nothing was ever from them again, and apart from some spurious folklore; their names, actions, and existence simply faded out of the memory of the living until occasionally someone felt like they were being watched from the banks or the forest. That sense of uneasy closeness that made people gather up their children in fear and scurry back inside. In some small way they will always be there but not there.

14

When he woke, he could sense that he was in a tunnel. But he didn't think he needed to be afraid. Whilst he could sense the tunnel due to the acoustic and proximity to his breath, this seemed to be a warm tunnel, one of safety.

There was a low-level rumbling coming from somewhere and occasionally he could hear voices. As he tried to raise his head and a loud piercing voice shrieked at him to lay still. Now he panicked. A few seconds later and after a series of bleeps and more whirring noises, bright lights blinded him, and the tunnel disappeared from before his face.

As his focus returned, he could see the instantly recognisable uniforms of the NHS doctors and nurses. Obviously, he was in hospital, but why?

After a few snide comments from the MRI operator, he was pushed back to the ward and placed in a side room by himself. He could have guessed it was his room as there was nothing in it. No slippers or clothes; nothing but his charcoal grey jacket (which he fondly remembered taking from a rather obnoxious highways agency worker who took great delight in trashing his water purifying kit). Time in hospital has its own special laws of physics, sometimes hours and days fly by, but today was one of those days when someone seems to press the pause button with alarming regularity.

After what must have been three hours, two doctors dressed in scrubs slowly entered his room and closed the door. He could tell that things were just about to get real by the look in their eyes. In a little under 90 seconds, they had the news that would cut him to the core. He had an inoperable brain tumour which was growing exponentially.

Without even asking him whether he wanted to know, their best guess was that he had a few weeks at best to live. With that (and a few mutterings about palliative care and pain relief) they left the room never to be seen again.

His breathing started to race, and he could feel himself become sweaty and clammy. In an instant the five stages of grief rushed through the door and lined themselves at the foot of his bed ready to present themselves. What had he done so wrong? why him who asked nothing from nobody? There must be a treatment or cure, after all they can do anything nowadays?

Over the next few hours, it was the anger that kept welling up inside him. The injustice that he had so much more to do and achieve in life, the anger that he hadn't fully explained his creed to the world. The outrage that his life had been about giving to others and now it was to be snuffed out by becoming a dribbling inoperative mess in no time at all.

Over the next couple of days, they had at least been able to make him feel slightly more normal by increasing his protein levels and giving him some medication for the nausea. This helped focus his mind as to how the end would come about and how it was going to be him that dictated that end. The care team were great, but their focus now was about how to get him out of the hospital and into a palliative unit where he could be "comfortable" For him, this was not an option. The idea of whiling away his precious last few moments on this planet listening to whale humping music in a care home was not going to happen.

Once he had informed them of his decision to leave, things got a little flustered at the nurses' station. You see, normally when you are as sick as he was, then you are more of a product or thing that is logistically managed from one setting to another. You don't normally state that you are leaving especially when you have no formal home to go to.

Knowledge though, was on his side and he knew full well that so long as he had mental capacity to make that informed decision then there was thankfully but regretfully on their part, nothing they could do.

He also knew that there is a still an old law that allows someone to remain in the location that they die until such a time as they become a hazard to the health of others. Armed with this knowledge he began his planning for the final push to freedom.

About a week later and they had stabilized him enough to make him steadier on his feet and with a slight shuffle and drag of the heels, to be able to walk.

He signed the forms, took his huge bag of medication, and left the ward. Already his sense of liberation began to well up inside of him. You see, last time he was leaving this place it was in a state of frenzy and suspicion. Now he held his head up as *he* took the control, and *he* actioned the bid decisions of his life and ultimately death. As he left through the North entrance, he couldn't help but feel a certain sense of pity for the stream of people heading into the hospital. It wasn't that the care was bad, it wasn't, in fact it was excellent; it was more that they had conceded to the great narrative that we have in the country that your life and condition is defined by the way the State helps you. You are on the dole, and your value is less to society, you are old or sick and your value is less to society, your lifestyle is unorthodox... In fact, the only way that the narrative changes in your favour is when you are working and paying taxes!

He wasn't interested in that narrative (although he had to acknowledge that taxes paid for his care) he was more interested in the meta narrative which drew you out of yourself and societal norms to encourage you to see how you fit (or not) in the bigger cosmic order. Who was the one calling the beat to the dance of life that we all follow?

With every new scientific discovery, it enabled humanity to appreciate how much we don't know, how the universe is so much bigger than we ever thought and how, if we dare, we too can share in that cosmic dance.

The only thing that he had requested before he left the ward was the possibility of a lift from the patient transport company. The ward manager had seemed a kind and compassionate woman who has agreed to this and so once outside he boarded the white minibus that would be his last vehicular ride ever. The minibus was one of those that had been hollowed out to allow for wheelchair space and hydraulic lifts and this made it very tinny and fragile sounding. The state of the van though was of little concern to him, rather that it would take him to where he needed to be. It was apparent that the driver wasn't really in the mood for talking and this suited him fine. He gave direction to travel toward Farnham just off the A3 and so the rattling van (which was to become his hearse) left Portsmouth and headed north.

Within 25 minutes they had started to see signs for Bentley and he asked the driver to pull into the next layby. Curiously, the driver didn't seem phased by this at all, as if dropping seriously ill patients off by the side of a busy 'A' road with no obvious signs of onward travel was the norm!

As the minibus smoked its way out of the layby, he couldn't help but reflect on the analogy of that old crate and life. We start off in life with a new vehicle which is shiny and raring to go, but as life takes its toll it becomes worn and slower, then ultimately, it no longer serves its purpose, and we walk the rest of the way.

Once safely across the A3 he started to make his way southwest down the narrow country lanes stopping only to top up on the pain killers and some water which the hospital had provided him. Summer was turning more towards autumn, but it was still one of those days when the sun was high and with little in the way of wind, sometimes quite stifling. After about three miles he felt that he needed to rest for a while and so slid through a gap in the adjacent field and lay down for a while.

Once the function and energy of walking had subsided it gave his mind time to reflect on what was happening and more importantly why.

He didn't consider himself special or gifted in anyway, in fact other than living on the banks, his life was quite ordinary. But he did, and always had felt that he was called to bear witness to something, but he could never really figure our what that something was. It didn't really matter as death was knocking at the door and that moment to shine had probably gone forever. Maybe he had missed a God given opportunity somewhere down the line. Maybe he taken a left in life when he should have taken a right. Maybe God had changed his mind and chosen someone else instead?

His drowsiness was rudely interrupted by what can only be described as prehistoric noise. A shrill rasp seemed to come from nowhere and it took him more than a few seconds to respond to his fight or flight processes. Now back to his sense he quickly recognised the sound as coming from a non-native bird which could mean that he was close to Birdworld and close to his destination.

His vision had started to deteriorate, and he couldn't fathom as to whether this was due to his exhaustion or the natural course of his tumour growing rapidly inside his brain like an unwelcome guest. Either way his focus now was on getting to the water's edge. He had first stumbled across Frensham pond on the advice of another banker. It was large enough to have pockets of undergrowth that would allow for a banker to go undetected. It was also rich enough to provide pretty much whatever you wanted from nature's menu. The pond was initially constructed under the direction of the Bishop of Winchester (William De Raleigh) in the 13th century to provide a fish supply for Farnham castle. It was a beautiful and serene place with gently sloping sand banks which allowed for easy access in the summer months, and it was this ease of access he needed now more than ever.

When he finally found the spot of his demise, he laid back against the reed beds as the sun effortlessly dipped below the forest canopy. A few day walkers were making their way back to the car park and he had seen the park ranger preparing to close the grounds once more. As the people left, so did the noise and all he was left with was the sound of mother nature as she settled in for the night. The occasional stirring of a coot or a fish breaking the meniscus was only interrupted by the sound of an owl as it took to flight in search of another meal.

He was struggling now, and he knew that the end was near. He could hear his own death rattle within his chest as his lungs struggled to clear themselves and he knew his final push was moving ever closer. When he had stopped earlier, he had popped all his pills from their pouches and kept them loosely within his jacket pocket and with last bit of bottled water he took them all. First in 2's or 3's then in great handfuls just get the job done. He had never liked or entertained the idea of suicide before as he reasoned that this gift of life was not his to take. But now he figured that there was little difference between him taking them all at once or lying in a hospice bed spacing them out in acceptable intervals.

Within moments he began to feel their effects. First, waves of heat came over him, then sporadic moments of shuddering cold. With this he gently and quietly slipped into the water and began to wade further out. He could feel the warm water envelop his body and it supported his weight enough to allow him to lay on his back with his head tilted to one side.

The pond has no natural current but through the winds it does form a gentle rhythm and movement. As the fresh waters lapped his cheek, he could just make out the May flies as they danced in the air by the lakeside. There was a definite intent to their movement whilst at the same time it was sporadic and chaotic. Maybe this was his life in a micro level; one with intent yet held within a dance of chaos.

He could feel that his life was leaving him as he slipped further and further into the great abyss and release. Maybe Arthur was right, maybe all that humanity needed was truth, beauty and goodness to survive?

The bankers are still there, existing in a world just beyond your sight so perhaps as you drive along the next road look and look again real hard to see the world that is right in front of you.

His body was never found. Once he had slipped beneath the surface the undercurrent drew him and trapped him against the sluice gate. In life he had been anonymous, and this continued in death. Perhaps this was God's will that his impact on life be hidden? Perhaps this is true on most people that are born; we sense them, occasionally see them, but their footprints tread lightly in the world.

Printed in Great Britain
by Amazon

74783099R00051